DISCARDED

Mister Dash and the Cupcake Calamity

Monica Kulling

Illustrated by

Esperança Melo

Tundra Books

Published in Canada by Tundra Books, a division of Random House of Canada Limited,
One Toronto Street, Suite 300, Toronto, Ontario M5C 2V6

Published in the United States by Tundra Books of Northern New York,
P.O. Box 1030, Plattsburgh, New York 12901

Library of Congress Control Number: 2012934219

Library and Archives Canada Cataloguing in Publication

Kulling, Monica, 1952-
        Mister Dash and the cupcake calamity / Monica
Kulling ; illustrated by Esperança Melo.

ISBN 978-1-77049-396-4. — ISBN 978-1-77049-402-2 (EPUB)

        I. Melo, Esperança II. Title.

PS8571.U54M57 2013   jC813'.54   C2012-901560-1

We acknowledge the financial support of the Government of Canada through the Canada Book Fund and that of the
Government of Ontario through the Ontario Media Development Corporation's Ontario Book Initiative. We further
acknowledge the support of the Canada Council for the Arts and the Ontario Arts Council for our publishing program.

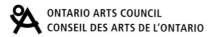

ONTARIO ARTS COUNCIL
CONSEIL DES ARTS DE L'ONTARIO

Edited by Sue Tate
Designed by Leah Springate
The artwork in this book was rendered in acrylic on paper.

www.tundrabooks.com

Printed and bound in China

1 2 3 4 5 6   18 17 16 15 14 13

For Sylvia Chan, cupcake queen, and for Esperança Melo, whose stunning illustrations for Merci Mister Dash! *inspired me to write a second story.*
M.K.

For the Natalias in my life – my mom, who loves color, and my sister and dear friend, who adores stories.
E.M.

Thank you, Nancy Ennis and Susan Hughes, for reading early drafts of this story and offering your helpful suggestions. Thank you, Sue Tate, for an exquisite edit.

Madame Croissant had a secret cupcake recipe. Croissant cupcakes were famous all over Europe, especially in France. She wanted them to be famous in North America too.

So Madame Croissant bought a third-hand van and painted *Cupcakes à Go-Go* on the side. She sewed a baker's hat for her well-mannered dog, Mister Dash, along with saddlebags for carrying the boxed treats. Then she baked and she baked.

"Mister Dash, you are now my delivery dog!" announced Madame Croissant.

Mister Dash found it difficult to put his best paw forward wearing saddlebags. He felt foolish carrying boxes in his mouth. And he was sure that the baker's hat made him look like a clown.

But dogs are faithful animals, and dogs made up of five different breeds are more faithful than most. So Mister Dash did not complain.

On the road, Madame Croissant's phone rang. *Brrring!*
"*Cupcakes à Go-Go,*" sang Madame Croissant.
"*Merci!* One dozen salted caramel and six rocky road."
And it *was* a rocky road with Madame Croissant at
the wheel. "Look out – here I come!" she shouted, her
hand on the horn. *Beep! Beeeep!*
When Madame Croissant swerved to avoid a
garbage can, the van ran up the curb and hit a stop
sign. The sign broke in two.

Sput. Sput. CLUNK. The van sputtered and died.

A mechanic came and looked under the hood. "This old buggy is on its last tires," she said.

"But you can fix it, yes?" asked Madame Croissant.

Suddenly Mister Dash had a thought. *If the van cannot be fixed . . . no more deliveries!* A smile lit up his face.

But . . . *VRROOOM!* The engine roared to life, and Madame Croissant backed into traffic. She made an artful U-turn, waved, and honked. *"Merci! Merci!" Beep! Beeeep!*

Today was baking day. Eggs, butter, sacks of flour, sugar, and cocoa crowded the counter. Boxes of chocolate and banana chips, dates, walnuts, sprinkles, and fancy marshmallows stood in rows on the table.

"*Bonjour, Grand-mère!*" called Daphne, slamming the front door. "I'm heeerrre!"

Madame Croissant was putting flour in her large sifter.

"*Bonjour, ma chérie,*" she sang back. "I knooow."

Mister Dash, wearing a disguise, was sneaking out the back door. But Daphne recognized him right away.

"Playtime, Mister Dash!" she shouted, stopping him in his tracks.

"Not today, *ma chérie*," interrupted Madame Croissant. "Mayor Chester Field has ordered five hundred cupcakes! I must make a good impression. And you will help me."

How exciting, Daphne thought. She had never baked anything before. She spotted the sifter. "I want to sift!" she exclaimed.

Daphne turned the handle like the little dynamo
she was. Clouds of flour flew everywhere.

"No more!" shouted Madame Croissant. "You
will measure. Mister Dash will sift."

Daphne tore open the boxes of chocolate and
banana chips for measuring. They flew like
sparks from a fire!

"*Fini!*" shouted Madame Croissant. "No more chips. You will mix. It is easy. Turn this switch on the machine. Like so."

The whisk went round and round in the bowl.

"Now push the dough down with this *spatule*," said Madame Croissant. "*Comme ça*. Like that."

Madame Croissant turned to grease the cupcake pans. *Whirrrr! Thwack!* A lump of dough hit the back of her head.

Whirrrr! Thwack! Whirrrr! Thwack! Thwack!

Dough stuck to the ceiling, the cupboards, and the walls.

"Oh, my goodness!" cried Madame Croissant.

"Yikes!" exclaimed Daphne.

Tout de suite, Mister Dash leapt into action. He turned off the mixer, and the dough stayed in the bowl.

Daphne licked the dough from her fingers. She was all smiles.

"Baking is fun. What can I do now, *Grand-mère?* I want an important job," she said, all in one breath.

Mister Dash was sweeping the floor. *What can Daphne do?*

"Boxes," said Madame Croissant brightly. "We need boxes. Without them, we cannot carry the cupcakes."

As it happened, Daphne was a talented box-maker. Her boxes were oddly shaped, and some didn't hold more than two cupcakes, but she got the job done and didn't make a mess – well, not much of one.

Everyone piled into the van. Cupcake boxes were stacked from floor to ceiling. Mister Dash curled up in the only bit of free space and soon fell asleep. Baking day was exhausting.

"We did it!" exclaimed Daphne.

"We are a good team," agreed Madame Croissant.

As she turned the key, the phone rang. It was the mayor. He was wondering when his cupcakes would arrive.

"We must dash," said Madame Croissant as she
stepped on the gas. *VRROOOM!*

When the van stopped at a light, the boxes teetered.
When it sped up, the boxes tottered. They rocked and
swayed while Mister Dash snoozed on.

"Look out – here we come!" shouted Madame
Croissant. *Beep! Beeeep!*

The cupcakes teetered, tottered, and finally toppled.

At the mayor's house, Madame Croissant
started to open the van doors. If she opened
them wide, the boxes would tumble into the
street. Five hundred cupcakes would crumble!
And so would Madame Croissant's dream.

"Oh, my goodness!" she cried. "The boxes are
falling out!"

"Mister Dash!" called Daphne. "We need
your help!"

Mister Dash woke with a start. He could hardly believe his eyes – the van was in total chaos. *What a calamity!* With his lab legs, he jumped into action and swiftly moved all the boxes away from the doors. He stacked them in neat rows so they would not fall again.

Then, Mister Dash carefully passed the boxes to Madame Croissant. He handed the small ones to Daphne. In the end, not one cupcake was lost.

"Bravo!" sang out Madame Croissant. "Mister Dash is a wonderful delivery dog!"

Daphne gave Mister Dash a big hug.

Mayor Chester Field's summer party was a delicious success. *Cupcakes à Go-Go* was soon the talk of the town.

Mister Dash continued to deliver cupcakes, but stopped wearing the baker's hat. It made all the difference.